Reginald Heber

Heber's Hymns

Reginald Heber

Heber's Hymns

ISBN/EAN: 9783337078980

Printed in Europe, USA, Canada, Australia, Japan

Cover: Foto ©Andreas Hilbeck / pixelio.de

More available books at **www.hansebooks.com**

Heber's Hymns

SECOND
ILLUSTRATED
EDITION.

LONDON.
SAMPSON LOW, SON, AND MARSTON.
CROWN BUILDINGS, FLEET STREET.

LONDON   PRINTED BY WILLIAM CLOWES AND SONS,
STAMFORD STREET AND CHARING CROSS.

BISHOP HEBER'S HYMNS are treasured as Sacred Household Words wherever the English language is spoken; not so much hitherto as a collection, but from their merit as separate Hymns; they are all favourites, and each has established its own claim to being so regarded without reference to their author or to each other's excellence.

No poet perhaps has commanded a more universal adoption of his sacred verse than *Reginald Heber*, and yet few poets are known less by a collection of their most popular productions; they would appear to be a valued possession of Christendom, yet scarcely recognised as the Hymns of one author. This arises partly from the devoted career of the Bishop in India superseding that of the poet, and partly from the unobtrusive way in which his own Hymns were given to the world in a collection formed by himself from ancient and modern writers to supply a want then felt for a Church Hymnal. The Bishop's own Hymns have outlived this publication in which he so unostentatiously incorporated them, and it is thought by the present publishers that a distinct edition of what the Bishop alone was author, will be acceptable to all admirers of devotional poetry, and at the same time, by adopting a permanent and ornamental form, afford them an opportunity to do honour to a memory ever to be revered.

The publication of this edition is undertaken with due regard to the interest of the surviving representative of the author, and with the sanction of Mr. Murray, who has published all the Bishop's works as well as his compilation of Hymns. As the plan upon which the Hymns were composed bears immediate reference to the Lessons of the Day, so has this leading idea been followed in the plan of illustration ; in many places a purely emblematic treatment has been found necessary where the reference has been more one of principle than incident.

The names of the various artists employed will form some guarantee that the designs have received careful study, and the whole have been engraved under the entire direction of Mr. James D. Cooper. It is hoped that their efforts will be esteemed to have accomplished the object of a suitable edition of these favourite Christian melodies.

CONTENTS.

LIST OF ILLUSTRATIONS.

ENGRAVED BY JAMES D. COOPER.

HOSANNA to the living Lord!
Hosanna to the incarnate Word!
To Christ, Creator. Saviour. King,
Let earth, let Heaven, Hosanna sing!
Hosanna! Lord! Hosanna in the highest!

Hosanna, Lord! Thine angels cry;
Hosanna, Lord! Thy saints reply;
Above, beneath us, and around,
The dead and living swell the sound:
Hosanna! Lord! Hosanna in the highest!

Advent Sunday.

Oh, Saviour! with protecting care,
Return to this Thy house of prayer!
Assembled in Thy sacred name,
Where we Thy parting promise claim!
    Hosanna! Lord! Hosanna in the highest!

But, chiefest, in our cleansed breast,
Eternal! bid Thy Spirit rest,
And make our secret soul to be
A temple pure, and worthy Thee!
    Hosanna! Lord! Hosanna in the highest!

So, in the last and dreadful day,
When earth and Heaven shall melt away,
Thy flock, redeem'd from sinful stain,
Shall swell the sound of praise again:
    Hosanna! Lord! Hosanna in the highest!

BEHOLD THE FIG TREE AND ALL THE TREES.

Second Sunday in Advent. —No. 1.

THE Lord will come! the earth shall quake,
The hills their fixed seat forsake ;
And, withering, from the vault of night
The stars withdraw their feeble light.

The Lord will come! but not the same
As once in lowly form He came,
A silent Lamb to slaughter led,
The bruised, the suffering, and the dead.

The Lord will come! a dreadful form,
With wreath of flame, and robe of storm,
On cherub wings, and wings of wind,
Anointed judge of human-kind!

Can this be He who wont to stray
A pilgrim on the world's highway ;
By power oppress'd, and mock'd by pride?
Oh God! is this the crucified?

Go, tyrants! to the rocks complain!
Go, seek the mountains cleft in vain!
But faith, victorious o'er the tomb,
Shall sing for joy—the Lord is come!

Second Sunday in Advent.—No. II.

—•.•—

Ṅ the sun and moon and stars
   Signs and wonders there shall be ;
Earth shall quake with inward wars,
   Nations with perplexity.

Soon shall ocean's hoary deep,
   Toss'd with stronger tempests, rise ;
Darker storms the mountains sweep,
   Redder lightning rend the skies.

Evil thoughts shall shake the proud,
   Racking doubt and restless fear ;
And, amid the thunder-cloud,
   Shall the Judge of men appear.

But though from that awful face
   Heaven shall fade and earth shall fly,
Fear not ye, His chosen race,
   Your redemption draweth nigh !

Third Sunday in Advent.

———

H Saviour, is Thy promise fled?
　　Nor longer might Thy grace endure,
To heal the sick and raise the dead,
　　And preach Thy Gospel to the poor?

Come, Jesus! come! return again;
　　With brighter beam Thy servants bless,
Who long to feel Thy perfect reign,
　　And share Thy kingdom's happiness!

BEHOLD I SEND MY MESSENGER BEFORE THY FACE

Third Sunday in Advent.

A feeble race, by passion driven,
　In darkness and in doubt we roam,
And lift our anxious eyes to Heaven,
　Our hope, our harbour, and our home !

Yet, 'mid the wild and wintry gale,
　When Death rides darkly o'er the sea,
And strength and earthly daring fail,
　Our prayers, Redeemer ! rest on Thee !

Come, Jesus ! come ! and, as of yore
　The prophet went to clear Thy way,
A harbinger Thy feet before,
　A dawning to Thy brighter day :

So now may grace with heavenly shower
　Our stony hearts for truth prepare ;
Sow in our souls the seed of power,
　Then come and reap Thy harvest there !

WHICH SHALL PREPARE THY WAY BEFORE THEE.

Fourth Sunday in Advent.

THE world is grown old, and her pleasures are past ;
The world is grown old, and her form may not last;
The world is grown old, and trembles for fear ;
For sorrows abound, and judgment is near !

The sun in the heaven is languid and pale ;
And feeble and few are the fruits of the vale ;
And the hearts of the nations fail them for fear,
For the world is grown old, and judgment is near !

The king on his throne, the bride in her bower,
The children of pleasure all feel the sad hour ;
The roses are faded, and tasteless the cheer,
For the world is grown old, and judgment is near :

The world is grown old ! —but should we complain,
Who have tried her and know that her promise is vain ?
Our heart is in Heaven, our home is not here,
And we look for our crown when judgment is near !

THE VOICE OF ONE CRYING IN THE WILDERNESS MAKE STRAIGHT THE WAY OF THE LORD.

CHRISTMAS DAY.

OH Saviour, whom this holy morn,
  Gave to our world below;
To mortal want and labour born,
  And more than mortal woe!

Incarnate Word! by every grief,
  By each temptation tried,
Who lived to yield our ills relief,
  And to redeem us died!

Christmas Day.

If gaily clothed and proudly fed
 In dangerous wealth we dwell;
Remind us of Thy manger bed
 And lowly cottage cell!

If prest by poverty severe,
 In envious want we pine,
Oh may the Spirit whisper near,
 How poor a lot was Thine!

Through fickle fortune's various scene
 From sin preserve us free!
Like us Thou hast a mourner been,
 May we rejoice with Thee!

St. Stephen's Day.

HE Son of God goes forth to war,
  A kingly crown to gain :
His blood-red banner streams afar !
  Who follows in His train ?

Who best can drink his cup of woe,
  Triumphant over pain,
Who patient bears his cross below,
  He follows in His train !

The martyr first, whose eagle eye
  Could pierce beyond the grave ;
Who saw his Master in the sky,
  And call'd on Him to save.

Like Him, with pardon on his tongue
  In midst of mortal pain,
He pray'd for them that did the wrong !
  Who follows in his train ?

10

St. Stephen's Day.

A glorious band, the chosen few
  On whom the Spirit came ;
Twelve valiant saints, their hope they knew,
  And mock'd the cross and flame.

They met the tyrant's brandish'd steel,
  The lion's gory mane ;
They bow'd their necks the death to feel !
  Who follows in their train ?

A noble army—men and boys,
  The matron and the maid,
Around the Saviour's throne rejoice,
  In robes of light array'd.

They climb'd the steep ascent of Heaven,
  Through peril, toil, and pain !
Oh God ! to us may grace be given
  To follow in their train !

Of whom the world was not worthy

St. John the Evangelist's Day.

—·•·—

OH God! who gav'st Thy servant grace,
　　Amid the storms of life distrest,
To look on Thine incarnate face,
　　And lean on Thy protecting breast:

To see the light that dimly shone,
　　Eclipsed for us in sorrow pale,
Pure Image of the Eternal One!
　　Through shadows of Thy mortal veil!

Be ours, O King of Mercy! still
　　To feel Thy presence from above,
And in Thy word, and in Thy will,
　　To hear Thy voice, and know Thy love:

And when the toils of life are done,
　　And nature waits Thy dread decree,
To find our rest beneath Thy throne,
　　And look, in humble hope, to Thee.

12

Innocents' Day.

WEEP not o'er thy children's tomb!
  O Rachel, weep not so;
The bud is cropt by martyrdom,
  The flower in heaven shall blow!

Firstlings of faith! the murderer's knife
  Has miss'd its deadliest aim:
The God for whom they gave their life,
  For them to suffer came!

Though feeble were their days and few,
  Baptized in blood and pain,
He knows them, whom they never knew,
  And they shall live again.

Then weep not o'er thy children's tomb:
  O Rachel, weep not so!
The bud is cropt by martyrdom,
  The flower in heaven shall blow!

13

Epiphany.

BRIGHTEST and best of the sons of the morning!
　　Dawn on our darkness and lend us Thine aid!
Star of the East, the horizon adorning,
　　Guide where our infant Redeemer is laid!

Cold on His cradle the dew-drops are shining,
　　Low lies His head with the beasts of the stall;
Angels adore Him in slumber reclining,
　　Maker and Monarch and Saviour of all!

Epiphany.

Say, shall we yield Him, in costly devotion,
  Odours of Edom and offerings divine?
Gems of the mountain and pearls of the ocean,
  Myrrh from the forest or gold from the mine?

Vainly we offer each ample oblation :
  Vainly with gifts would His favour secure :
Richer by far is the heart's adoration ;
  Dearer to God are the prayers of the poor.

Brightest and best of the sons of the morning !
  Dawn on our darkness and lend us Thine aid !
Star of the East, the horizon adorning,
  Guide where our infant Redeemer is laid !

First Sunday after Epiphany. No. 1.

BASH'D be all the boast of age !
Be hoary learning dumb !
Expounder of the mystic page,
Behold an Infant come !

Oh Wisdom, whose unfading power
Beside the Eternal stood,
To frame, in nature's earliest hour,
The land, the sky, the flood :

Yet didst not Thou disdain awhile
  An infant form to wear ;
To bless Thy mother with a smile,
  And lisp Thy falter'd prayer.

But in Thy Father's own abode,
  With Israel's elders round,
Conversing high with Israel's God
  Thy chiefest joy was found.

So may our youth adore Thy name !
  And, Saviour, deign to bless
With fostering grace the timid flame
  Of early holiness !

First Sunday after Epiphany.   No. II.

··

BY cool Siloam's shady rill
    How sweet the lily grows!
How sweet the breath beneath the hill
    Of Sharon's dewy rose!

Lo! such the child whose early feet
    The paths of peace have trod;
Whose secret heart, with influence sweet,
    Is upward drawn to God!

By cool Siloam's shady rill
    The lily must decay;
The rose that blooms beneath the hill
    Must shortly fade away.

And soon, too soon, the wintry hour
    Of man's maturer age
Will shake the soul with sorrow's power,
    And stormy passion's rage!

O Thou, whose infant feet were found
    Within Thy Father's shrine!
Whose years, with changeless virtue
        crown'd,
    Were all alike Divine;

First Sunday after Epiphany.

Dependent on Thy bounteous breath,
 We seek Thy grace alone,
In childhood, manhood, age, and death,
 To keep us still thine own.

Second Sunday after Epiphany. No. 1.

O! hand of bounty, largely spread,
By whom our every want is fed,
Whate'er we touch, or taste, or see,
We owe them all, oh Lord! to Thee:
The corn, the oil, the purple wine,
Are all Thy gifts, and only Thine!

The stream Thy word to nectar dyed,
The bread Thy blessing multiplied,
The stormy wind, the whelming flood,
That silent at Thy mandate stood,
How well they knew Thy voice Divine,
Whose works they were, and only Thine!

Though now no more on earth we trace
Thy footsteps of celestial grace,
Obedient to Thy word and will
We seek Thy daily mercy still;
Its blessed beams around us shine,
And Thine we are, and only Thine.

20

Second Sunday after Epiphany.—No. II.

INCARNATE Word, who, wont to dwell
In lowly shape and cottage cell,
Didst not refuse a guest to be,
At Cana's poor festivity :

Oh, when our soul from care is free,
Then, Saviour, may we think on Thee,
And, seated at the festal board,
In fancy's eye behold the Lord.

Then may we seem, in fancy's ear,
Thy manna-dropping tongue to hear,
And think,—even now, Thy searching gaze
Each secret of our soul surveys !

So may such joy, chastised and pure,
Beyond the bounds of earth endure ;
Nor pleasure in the wounded mind
Shall leave a rankling sting behind !

Second Sunday after Epiphany.　No. III.

— ❖ —

WHEN on her Maker's bosom
　　The new-born earth was laid,
And Nature's opening blossom
　　Its fairest bloom display'd;

When all with fruit and flowers
　　The laughing soil was drest,
And Eden's fragrant bowers
　　Received their human guest;

No sin his face defiling,
　　The heir of nature stood,
And God, benignly smiling,
　　Beheld that all was good!

Yet, in that hour of blessing,
　　A single want was known;
A wish the heart distressing;
　　For Adam was alone!

Oh God of pure affection!
　　By men and saints adored,
Who gavest Thy protection
　　To Cana's nuptial board;

May such Thy bounties ever
　　To wedded love be shown,
And no rude hand dissever
　　Whom Thou hast link'd in one!

Third Sunday after Epiphany.

LORD! whose love, in power excelling,
　Wash'd the leper's stain away,
Jesus! from Thy heavenly dwelling,
　Hear us, help us, when we pray!

From the filth of vice and folly,
　From infuriate passion's rage,
Evil thoughts and hopes unholy,
　Heedless youth and selfish age;

From the lusts whose deep pollutions
　Adam's ancient taint disclose,
From the Tempter's dark intrusions,
　Restless doubt and blind repose;

From the miser's cursed treasure,
　From the drunkard's jest obscene,
From the world, its pomp and pleasure,
　Jesus! Master! make us clean!

23

Fourth Sunday after Epiphany. No. 1.

WHEN through the torn sail the wild tempest is streaming,
  When o'er the dark wave the red lightning is gleaming,
Nor hope lends a ray the poor seamen to cherish,
We fly to our Maker "Help, Lord! or we perish!"

Oh Jesus! once toss'd on the breast of the billow,
Aroused by the shriek of despair from Thy pillow,
Now, seated in glory, the mariner cherish,
Who cries in his danger "Help, Lord! or we perish!"

24

_____ --

Fourth Sunday after Epiphany.

And oh, when the whirlwind of passion is raging,
When hell in our heart his wild warfare is waging,
Arise in Thy strength Thy redeemed to cherish,
Rebuke the destroyer—"Help, Lord! or we perish!"

Fourth Sunday after Epiphany.—No. II.

THE winds were howling o'er the deep,
    Each wave a wat'ry hill,
The Saviour waken'd from His sleep,
    He spake and all was still.

The madman in a tomb had made
    His mansion of despair;
Woe to the traveller who stray'd
    With heedless footstep there!

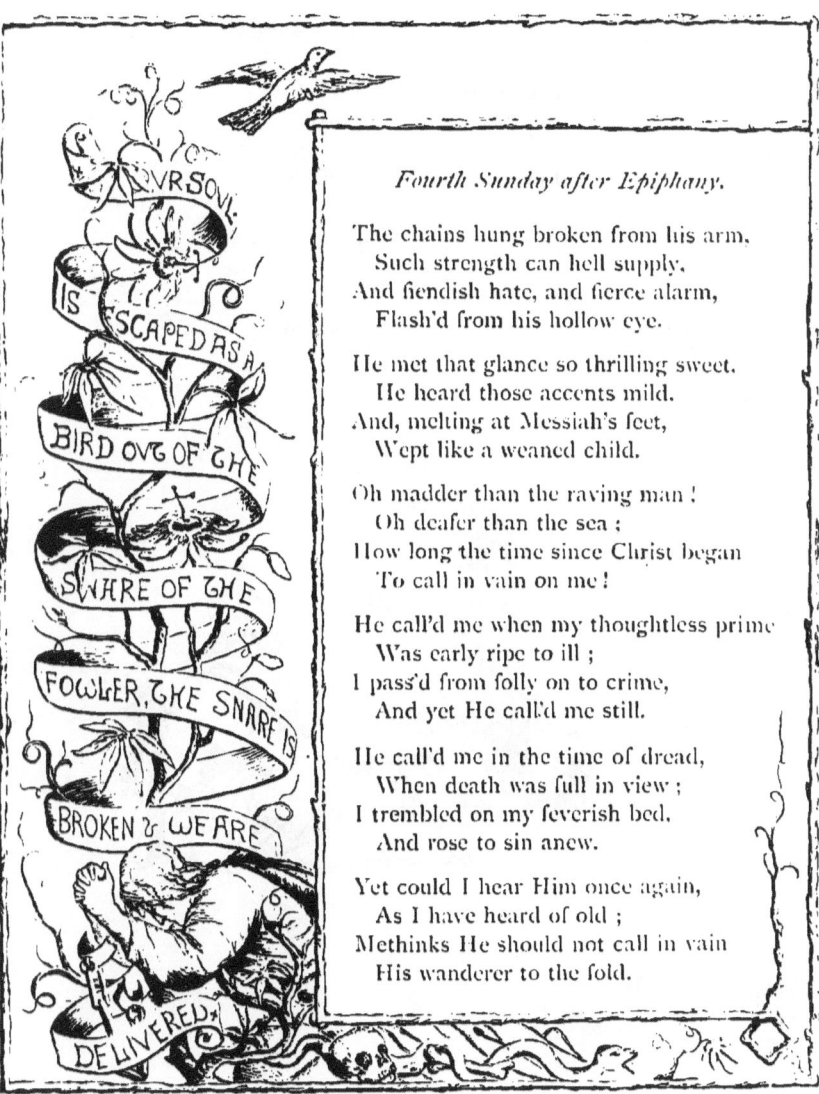

OUR SOUL IS ESCAPED AS A BIRD OVT OF THE SNARE OF THE FOWLER, THE SNARE IS BROKEN & WE ARE DELIVERED.

Fourth Sunday after Epiphany.

The chains hung broken from his arm,
   Such strength can hell supply,
And fiendish hate, and fierce alarm,
   Flash'd from his hollow eye.

He met that glance so thrilling sweet,
   He heard those accents mild,
And, melting at Messiah's feet,
   Wept like a weaned child.

Oh madder than the raving man !
   Oh deafer than the sea :
How long the time since Christ began
   To call in vain on me !

He call'd me when my thoughtless prime
   Was early ripe to ill ;
I pass'd from folly on to crime,
   And yet He call'd me still.

He call'd me in the time of dread,
   When death was full in view ;
I trembled on my feverish bed,
   And rose to sin anew.

Yet could I hear Him once again,
   As I have heard of old ;
Methinks He should not call in vain
   His wanderer to the fold.

Fourth Sunday after Epiphany.

Oh Thou that every thought canst know,
  And answer every prayer;
Oh give me sickness, want, or woe,
  But snatch me from despair!

My struggling will by grace control,
  Renew my broken vow!
What blessed light breaks on my soul?
  O God! I hear Thee now.

Septuagesima Sunday.

— ❖ —

THE God of Glory walks His round,
　　From day to day, from year to year,
And warns us each with awful sound,
　　" No longer stand ye idle here !

" Ye whose young cheeks are rosy bright,
　　Whose hands are strong, whose hearts are clear,
Waste not of hope the morning light !
　　Ah fools ! why stand ye idle here ?

29

Septuagesima Sunday.

" Oh, as the griefs ye would assuage
That wait on life's declining year,
Secure a blessing for your age,
And work your Maker's business here !

" And ye, whose locks of scanty grey
Foretell your latest travail near,
How swiftly fades your worthless day !
And stand ye yet so idle here ?

" One hour remains, there is but one !
But many a shriek and many a tear
Through endless years the guilt must moan
Of moments lost and wasted here !" ·

Oh Thou, by all Thy works adored,
To whom the sinner's soul is dear,
Recall us to Thy vineyard, Lord !
And grant us grace to please Thee here !

30

Sexagesima Sunday.

O H God! by whom the seed is given;
By whom the harvest blest;
Whose word, like manna shower'd from
Heaven,
Is planted in our breast;

Preserve it from the passing feet,
And plunderers of the air;
The sultry sun's intenser heat,
And weeds of worldly care!

Though buried deep or thinly strewn,
Do Thou Thy grace supply;
The hope in earthly furrows sown
Shall ripen in the sky!

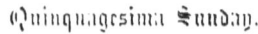

Quinquagesima Sunday.

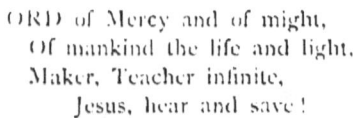

LORD of Mercy and of might,
Of mankind the life and light,
Maker, Teacher infinite,
　　Jesus, hear and save!

Who, when sin's primæval doom
Gave creation to the tomb,
Didst not scorn a Virgin's womb,
　　Jesus, hear and save!

76

Quinquagesima Sunday.

Strong Creator, Saviour mild,
Humbled to a mortal child,
Captive, beaten, bound, reviled,
    Jesus, hear and save!

Throned above celestial things,
Borne aloft on angels' wings,
Lord of lords, and King of kings,
    Jesus, hear and save!

Soon to come to earth again,
Judge of angels and of men,
Hear us now, and hear us then,
    Jesus, hear and save!

Third Sunday in Lent.

VIRGIN-BORN! we bow before Thee!
  Blessed was the womb that bore Thee!
Mary, mother meek and mild,
Blessed was she in her child!

Blessed was the breast that fed Thee!
Blessed was the hand that led Thee:
Blessed was the parent's eye
That watch'd Thy slumbering infancy!

Third Sunday in Lent.

Blessed she by all creation,
Who brought forth the world's Salvation!
And blessed they, for ever blest,
Who love Thee most and serve Thee best!

Virgin-born! we bow before Thee!
Blessed was the womb that bore Thee!
Mary, mother meek and mild,
Blessed was she in her child!

Fourth Sunday in Lent.

—·•—

KING of earth and air and sea!
The hungry ravens cry to Thee;
To Thee the scaly tribes that sweep
The bosom of the boundless deep;

To Thee the lions roaring call,
The common Father, kind to all!
Then grant Thy servants, Lord! we pray,
Our daily bread from day to day!

The fishes may for food complain;
The ravens spread their wings in vain:
The roaring lions lack and pine!
But, God! Thou carest still for Thine!

Fourth Sunday in Lent.

Thy bounteous hand with food can bless
The bleak and lonely wilderness;
And Thou hast taught us, Lord! to pray
For daily bread from day to day!

And oh, when through the wilds we roam
That part us from our heavenly home;
When lost in danger, want, and woe,
Our faithless tears begin to flow;

Do Thou Thy gracious comfort give,
By which alone the soul may live;
And grant Thy servants, Lord! we pray,
The bread of life from day to day!

Fifth Sunday in Lent.

OH Thou whom neither time nor space
  Can circle in, unseen, unknown,
Nor faith in boldest flight can trace,
  Save through Thy Spirit and Thy Son!

And Thou that from Thy bright abode,
  To us in mortal weakness shown,
Didst graft the manhood into God,
  Eternal, co-eternal Son!

And Thou, whose unction from on high
  By comfort, light, and love is known!
Who, with the parent Deity,
  Dread Spirit! art for ever One!

Great First and Last! Thy blessing give!
  And grant us faith, Thy gift alone,
To love and praise Thee while we live,
  And do whate'er Thou wouldst have done!

Sixth Sunday in Lent.

THE Lord of Might, from Sinai's brow,
  Gave forth His voice of thunder!
And Israel lay on earth below,
  Outstretch'd in fear and wonder.
Beneath His feet was pitchy night,
And at His left hand and His right,
  The rocks were sent asunder!

The Lord of Love, on Calvary,
  A meek and suffering stranger,
Upraised to Heaven His languid eye,
  In nature's hour of danger.
For us He bore the weight of woe,
For us He gave His blood to flow,
  And met His Father's anger.

The Lord of Love, the Lord of Might,
  The King of all created,
Shall back return to claim His right,
  On clouds of glory seated;
With trumpet-sound and angel-song,
And hallelujahs loud and long
  O'er death and hell defeated!

Good Friday.

OH more than merciful! whose bounty gave
  Thy guiltless self to glut the greedy grave!
Whose heart was rent to pay Thy people's price!
The great High-priest at once and sacrifice!
Help, Saviour, by Thy cross and crimson stain,
Nor let Thy glorious blood be spilt in vain!

Good Friday.

When sin with flowery garland hides her dart,
When tyrant force would daunt the sinking heart,
When fleshly lust assails, or worldly care,
Or the soul flutters in the fowler's snare,—
Help, Saviour, by Thy cross and crimson stain,
Nor let Thy glorious blood be spilt in vain!

And chiefest then, when Nature yields the strife,
And mortal darkness wraps the gate of life;
When the poor spirit, from the tomb set free,
Sinks at Thy feet and lifts its hope to Thee, —
Help, Saviour, by Thy cross and crimson stain,
Nor let Thy glorious blood be spilt in vain.

Easter Day.

—◆—

OD is gone up with a merry noise
Of saints that sing on high,
With His own right hand and His holy arm
He hath won the victory!

Now empty are the courts of Death,
And crush'd thy sting, Despair;
And roses bloom in the desert tomb,
For Jesus hath been there!

43

And He hath tamed the strength of Hell,
  And dragg'd him through the sky,
And captive behind His chariot wheel,
  He hath bound Captivity.

God is gone up with a merry noise
  Of saints that sing on high ;
With His own right hand and His holy arm
  He hath won the victory !

Fifth Sunday after Easter.

LIFE nor Death shall us dissever
From His love who reigns for ever:
Will He fail us? Never! never!
    When to Him we cry!

Sin may seek to snare us,
Fury Passion tear us!
Doubt and Fear, and grim Despair,
    Their fangs against us try;

But His might shall still defend us,
And His blessed Son befriend us,
And His Holy Spirit send us
    Comfort ere we die!

45

Ascension Day and Sunday after.

————⋄⋄————

IT Thou on my right hand, my Son!" saith the
    Lord.
" Sit Thou on my right hand, my Son!
      Till in the fatal hour
      Of my wrath and my power,
Thy foes shall be a footstool to Thy throne!"

" Prayer shall be made to Thee, my Son!" saith
    the Lord.
" Prayer shall be made to Thee, my Son!
      From earth and air and sea,
      And all that in them be,
Which Thou for Thine heritage hast won!"

" Daily be Thou praised, my Son!" saith the Lord.
" Daily be Thou praised, my Son!
      And all that live and move,
      Let them bless Thy bleeding love,
And the work which Thy worthiness hath done!"

46

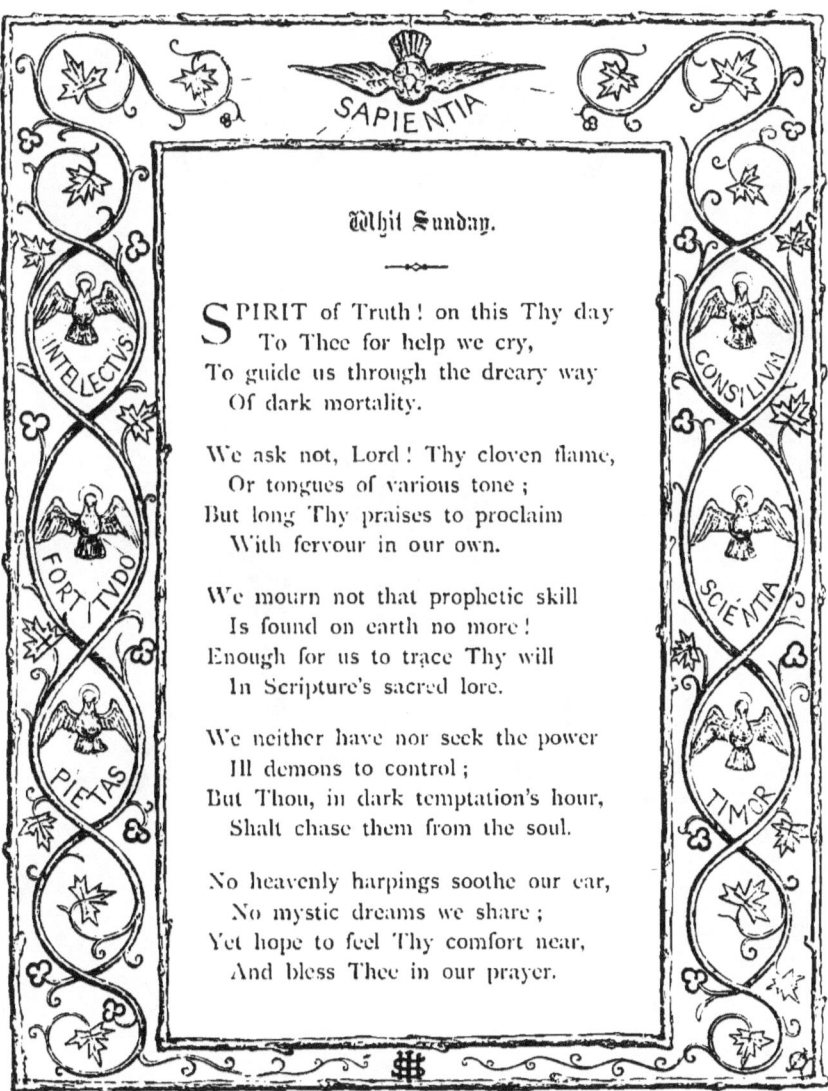

SAPIENTIA

Whit Sunday.

SPIRIT of Truth! on this Thy day
　　To Thee for help we cry,
To guide us through the dreary way
　　Of dark mortality.

We ask not, Lord! Thy cloven flame,
　　Or tongues of various tone;
But long Thy praises to proclaim
　　With fervour in our own.

We mourn not that prophetic skill
　　Is found on earth no more!
Enough for us to trace Thy will
　　In Scripture's sacred lore.

We neither have nor seek the power
　　Ill demons to control;
But Thou, in dark temptation's hour,
　　Shalt chase them from the soul.

No heavenly harpings soothe our ear,
　　No mystic dreams we share;
Yet hope to feel Thy comfort near,
　　And bless Thee in our prayer.

INTELECTVS

FORTITVDO

PIETAS

CONSILIVM

SCIENTIA

TIMOR

Whit Sunday.

When tongues shall cease and power decay,
  And knowledge empty prove,
Do Thou Thy trembling servants stay
  With Faith, with Hope, with Love!

Trinity Sunday.

HOLY, holy, holy, Lord God Almighty!
    Early in the morning our song shall rise to Thee;
Holy, holy, holy, merciful and mighty!
    God in three persons, blessed Trinity!

Holy, holy, holy! all Thy saints adore Thee,
    Casting down their golden crowns around the glassy sea!
Cherubim and seraphim falling down before Thee,
    Which wert and art and evermore shalt be!

Holy, holy, holy! Though the darkness hide Thee,
    Though the eye of sinful man Thy glory may not see,
Only Thou art holy, there is none beside Thee,
    Perfect in power, in love, and purity!

Holy, holy, holy! Lord God Almighty!
    All Thy works shall praise Thy name in earth and sky
      and sea.
Holy, holy, holy! merciful and mighty!
    God in three persons, blessed Trinity!

First Sunday after Trinity.—No. I.

ROOM for the proud! Ye sons of clay,
From far his sweeping pomp survey,
Nor, rashly curious, clog the way
    His chariot wheels before!

Lo! with what scorn his lofty eye
Glances o'er age and poverty,
And bids intruding conscience fly
    Far from his palace door!

Room for the proud! but slow the feet
That bear his coffin down the street:
And dismal seems his winding sheet
    Who purple lately wore!

Ah! where must now his spirit fly
In naked, trembling agony;
Or how shall he for mercy cry,
    Who show'd it not before!

Room for the proud! in ghastly state
The Lords of hell his coming wait,
And flinging wide the dreadful gate
    That shuts to ope no more,

"Lo here with us the seat," they cry,
"For him who mock'd at poverty,
And bade intruding conscience fly
    Far from his palace door."

WHAT·IS·YOUR·LIFE· IT·IS·E/EN·A·VAPOUR·THAT·
APPEARETH·FOR·A·LITTLE·TIME·AND·THEN·
VANISHETH AWAY

First Sunday after Trinity.—No. II.

THE feeble pulse, the gasping breath,
    The clenched teeth, the glazed eye,
Are these thy sting, thou dreadful Death?
    O Grave, are these thy victory!

The mourners by our parting bed,
    The wife, the children weeping nigh,
The dismal pageant of the dead,
    These, these are not thy victory!

But from the much-loved world to part,
    Our lust untamed, our spirit high,
All nature struggling at the heart,
    Which, dying, feels it dare not die!

To dream through life a gaudy dream
    Of pride and pomp and luxury,
Till waken'd by the nearer gleam
    Of burning boundless agony;

To meet o'er soon our angry King,
  Whose love we pass'd unheeded by ;
Lo this, O Death, thy deadliest sting !
  O Grave, and this thy victory !

O Searcher of the secret heart,
  Who deign'd for sinful man to die !
Restore us ere the spirit part,
  Nor give to Hell the victory !

Second Sunday after Trinity.

FORTH from the dark and stormy sky,
Lord, to Thine altar's shade we fly;
Forth from the world, its hope and fear,
Saviour, we seek Thy shelter here:
Weary and weak, Thy grace we pray:
Turn not, O Lord! Thy guests away!

Long have we roam'd in want and pain,
Long have we sought Thy rest in vain!
Wilder'd in doubt, in darkness lost,
Long have our souls been tempest-tost:
Low at Thy feet our sins we lay;
Turn not, O Lord! Thy guests away!

54

Third Sunday after Trinity.

THERE was joy in Heaven!
　　There was joy in Heaven!
When this goodly world to frame
The Lord of might and mercy came:
Shouts of joy were heard on high,
And the stars sang from the sky—
　" Glory to God in Heaven!"

There was joy in Heaven!
There was joy in Heaven!
When the billows, heaving dark,
Sank around the stranded ark,
And the rainbow's watery span
Spake of mercy, hope to man,
　And peace with God in Heaven!

55

Third Sunday after Trinity.

There was joy in Heaven!
There was joy in Heaven!
When of love the midnight beam
Dawn'd on the towers of Bethlehem;
And along the echoing hill
Angels sang —"On earth good-will,
    And glory in the Heaven!"

Fourth Sunday after Trinity.

PRAISED the earth, in beauty seen
  With garlands gay of various green ;
  I praised the sea, whose ample field
  Shone glorious as a silver shield ;
  And earth and ocean seem'd to say,
  " Our beauties are but for a day ! "

  I praised the sun, whose chariot roll'd
  On wheels of amber and of gold ;
  I praised the moon, whose softer eye
  Gleam'd sweetly through the summer sky
  And moon and sun in answer said,
  " Our days of light are numbered ! "

57

Fourth Sunday after Trinity.

O God! O Good beyond compare!
If thus Thy meaner works are fair!
If thus Thy bounties gild the span
Of ruin'd earth and sinful man,
How glorious must the mansion be
Where Thy redeem'd shall dwell with Thee!

Fifth Sunday after Trinity.

CREATOR of the rolling flood!
   On whom Thy people hope alone :
Who cam'st by water and by blood,
   For man's offences to atone :

Who from the labours of the deep
   Didst set Thy servant Peter free,
To feed on earth Thy chosen sheep,
   And build an endless church to Thee.

Grant us, devoid of worldly care,
   And leaning on Thy bounteous hand,
To seek Thy help in humble prayer,
   And on Thy sacred rock to stand :

And when, our livelong toil to crown,
   Thy call shall set the spirit free,
To cast with joy our burthen down,
   And rise, O Lord ! and follow Thee !

Seventh Sunday after Trinity.

— ·•· —

WHEN Spring unlocks the flowers to paint the laughing soil ;
 When Summer's balmy showers refresh the mower's toil ;
When Winter binds in frosty chains the fallow and the flood,
In God the earth rejoiceth still, and owns his Maker good.

The birds that wake the morning, and those that love the shade ;
The winds that sweep the mountain or lull the drowsy glade,
The sun that from his amber bower rejoiceth on his way,
The moon and stars, their Master's name in silent pomp display.

Seventh Sunday after Trinity.

Shall man, the lord of Nature, expectant of the sky,
Shall man, alone unthankful, his little praise deny?
No, let the year forsake his course, the seasons cease to be,
Thee, Master, must we always love, and, Saviour, honour Thee.

The flowers of Spring may wither, the hope of Summer fade,
The Autumn droop in winter, the birds forsake the shade :
The winds be lull'd—the sun and moon forget their old decree,
But we in Nature's latest hour, O Lord! will cling to Thee.

Tenth Sunday after Trinity.

— · · —

ERUSALEM, Jerusalem! enthroned once on high,
Thou favour'd home of God on earth, thou heaven below the sky;
Now brought to bondage with thy sons, a curse and grief to see,
Jerusalem, Jerusalem! our tears shall flow for thee.

Oh! hadst thou known thy day of grace, and flock'd beneath
the wing
Of Him who call'd thee lovingly, thine own anointed King,
Then had the tribes of all the world gone up thy pomp to see,
And glory dwelt within thy gates, and all thy sons been free.

62

" And who art thou that mournest me ?" replied the ruin grey,
" And fear'st not rather that thyself may prove a cast-away ?
I am a dried and abject branch, my place is given to thee ;
But woe to every barren graft of thy wild olive-tree !

" Our day of grace is sunk in night, our time of mercy spent,
For heavy was my children's crime, and strange their punishment ;
Yet gaze not idly on our fall, but, sinner, warned be :
Who spared not His chosen seed may send His wrath on thee !

" Our day of grace is sunk in night, thy noon is in its prime ;
Oh, turn and seek thy Saviour's face in this accepted time !
So, Gentile, may Jerusalem a lesson prove to thee,
And in the new Jerusalem thy home for ever be !"

Thirteenth Sunday after Trinity.

—◦•◦—

"HO yonder on the desert heath,
    Complains in feeble tone?"
—"A pilgrim in the vale of death,
    Faint, bleeding, and alone!"

"How cam'st thou to this dismal strand
    Of danger, grief, and shame?"
—"From blessed Sion's holy land,
    By Folly led, I came!"

" What ruffian hand hath stript thee bare ?
   Whose fury laid thee low ?"
—" Sin for my footsteps twined her snare,
   And Death has dealt the blow ! "

" Can art no medicine for thy wound,
   Nor nature strength supply?"
—" They saw me bleeding on the ground,
   And pass'd in silence by !"

" But, sufferer ! is no comfort near
   Thy terrors to remove?"
—" There is to whom my soul was dear,
   But I have scorn'd His love."

" What if His hand were nigh to save
   From endless Death thy days ? "
—" The soul He ransom'd from the grave
   Should live but to His praise ! "

" Rise then, oh rise !· His health embrace,
   With heavenly strength renew'd ;
And, such as is thy Saviour's grace,
   Such be thy gratitude ! "

Fifteenth Sunday after Trinity.

LO the lilies of the field,
How their leaves instruction yield!
Hark to Nature's lesson given
By the blessed birds of Heaven!
Every bush and tufted tree
Warbles sweet philosophy:
" Mortal, fly from doubt and sorrow;
God provideth for the morrow!

" Say, with richer crimson glows
The kingly mantle than the rose?
Say, have kings more wholesome fare
Than we, poor citizens of air?
Barns nor hoarded grain have we,
Yet we carol merrily.
Mortal, fly from doubt and sorrow!
God provideth for the morrow!

" One there lives whose guardian eye
Guides our humble destiny;
One there lives who, Lord of all,
Keeps our feathers lest they fall:
Pass we blithely then the time,
Fearless of the snare and lime,
Free from doubt and faithless sorrow;
God provideth for the morrow!"

Sixteenth Sunday after Trinity.

AKE not, O mother, sounds of lamentation !
   Weep not, O widow, weep not hopelessly !
Strong is His arm, the Bringer of Salvation,
   Strong is the Word of God to succour thee ✛

67

Sixteenth Sunday after Trinity.

Bear forth the cold corpse, slowly, slowly bear him :
  Hide his pale features with the sable pall :
Chide not the sad one wildly weeping near him :
  Widow'd and childless, she has lost her all !

Why pause the mourners ? Who forbids our weeping?
  Who the dark pomp of sorrow has delay'd ?
" Set down the bier,—he is not dead but sleeping !
  Young man, arise ; " He spake, and was obey'd !

Change then, O sad one ! grief to exultation :
  Worship and fall before Messiah's knee :
Strong was His arm, the Bringer of Salvation ;
  Strong was the Word of God to succour thee !

ON THE RESURRECTION.
I AM AND THE LIFE

Nineteenth Sunday after Trinity.

O H blest were the accents of early creation,
    When the Word of Jehovah came down from above ;
In the clods of the earth to infuse animation,
    And wake their cold atoms to life and to love !

And mighty the tones which the firmament rended,
    When on wheels of the thunder, and wings of the wind,
By lightning, and hail, and thick darkness attended,
    He utter'd on Sinai His laws to mankind.

And sweet was the voice of the First-born of Heaven,
    (Though poor His apparel, though earthly His form,)
Who said to the mourner, " Thy sins are forgiven !"
    " Be whole !" to the sick, and " Be still !" to the storm.

Nineteenth Sunday after Trinity.

Oh Judge of the World! when array'd in Thy glory,
  Thy summons again shall be heard from on high,
While Nature stands trembling and naked before Thee,
  And waits on Thy sentence to live or to die;

When the Heaven shall fly fast from the sound of Thy thunder,
  And the Sun, in Thy lightnings, grow languid and pale,
And the Sea yield her dead, and the Tomb cleave asunder,
  In the hour of Thy terrors, let mercy prevail!

———◆———

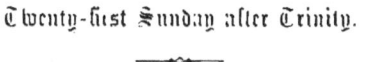

THE sound of war! In earth and air
　　The volleying thunders roll :
Their fiery darts the fiends prepare,
And dig the pit, and spread the snare,
　Against the Christian's soul.
The tyrant's sword, the rack, the flame,
　　The scorner's serpent tone,
Of bitter doubt the barbed aim,
All, all conspire his heart to tame :
Force, fraud, and hellish fires assail
The rivets of his heavenly mail,
　　Amidst his foes alone.

Gods of the world! ye warrior host
　　Of darkness and of air,
In vain is all your impious boast,
In vain each missile lightning tost,
　In vain the tempter's snare!
Though fast and far your arrows fly,
　　Though mortal nerve and bone
Shrink in convulsive agony,
The Christian can your rage defy :
Towers o'er his head salvation's crest,
Faith like a buckler guards his breast,
　　Undaunted, though alone.

THE·WHOLE·ARMOUR
PUT·ON OF·GOD.

'Tis past! 'tis o'er! in foul defeat
  The Demon host are fled!
Before the Saviour's mercy-seat,
  (His live-long work of faith complete,)
    Their conqueror bends his head.
"The spoils Thyself hast gained, Lord!
    I lay before Thy throne:
Thou wert my rock, my shield, my sword;
My trust was in Thy name and word:
'Twas in Thy strength my heart was strong;
Thy Spirit went with mine along;
    How was I then alone?"

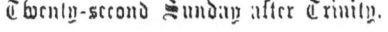

Twenty-second Sunday after Trinity.

God! my sins are manifold, against my life they cry,
And all my guilty deeds forgone, up to Thy temple fly;
Wilt Thou release my trembling soul, that to despair is driven?
" Forgive!" a blessed voice replied, "and thou shalt be
forgiven!"

My foemen, Lord! are fierce and fell, they spurn me in their
pride,
They render evil for my good, my patience they deride;
Arise, oh King; and be the proud to righteous ruin driven!
" Forgive!" an awful answer came, "as thou wouldst be
forgiven!"

Seven times, O Lord! I pardon'd them, seven times they
sinn'd again;
They practise still to work me woe, they triumph in my pain:
But let them dread my vengeance now, to just resentment
driven!
" Forgive!" the voice of thunder spake, "or never be forgiven!"

Twenty-third Sunday after Trinity.

FROM foes that would the land devour ;
From guilty pride, and lust of power ;
From wild sedition's lawless hour ;
From yoke of slavery :
From blinded zeal by faction led ;
From giddy change by fancy bred ;
From poisonous error's serpent head,
Good Lord ! preserve us free !

Defend, O God ! with guardian hand,
The laws and ruler of our land,
And grant our Church Thy grace to stand
In faith and unity !
The Spirit's help of Thee we crave,
That Thou whose blood was shed to save,
May'st at Thy second coming have
A flock to welcome Thee !

Twenty-fourth Sunday after Trinity.

— ∙⋄∙ —

conquer and to save, the Son of God
Came to His own in great humility,
Who wont to ride on cherub-wings abroad,
And round Him wrap the mantle of the sky.
The mountains bent their necks to form His road :
The clouds dropt down their fatness from on high :
Beneath His feet the wild waves softly flow'd,
And the winds kiss'd His garment tremblingly !

The grave unbolted half his grisly door,
(For darkness and the deep had heard His fame,
Nor longer might their ancient rule endure ;)
The mightiest of mankind stood hush'd and tame :
And, trooping on strong wing, His angels came
To work His will, and kingdom to secure :
No strength He needed save His Father's name :
Babes were His heralds, and His friends the poor !

St. James's Day.

T HOUGH sorrows rise, and dangers roll
In waves of darkness o'er my soul,
Though friends are false and love decays,
And few and evil are my days,
Though conscience, fiercest of my foes,
Swells with remember'd guilt my woes,
Yet ev'n in nature's utmost ill,
I love Thee, Lord! I love Thee still!

Though Sinai's curse, in thunder dread,
Peals o'er mine unprotected head,
And memory points, with busy pain,
To grace and mercy given in vain,
Till nature, shrinking in the strife,
Would fly to hell to 'scape from life,
Though every thought has power to kill,
I love Thee, Lord! I love Thee still!

Oh, by the pangs Thyself hast borne,
The ruffian's blow, the tyrant's scorn;
By Sinai's curse, whose dreadful doom
Was buried in Thy guiltless tomb:
By these my pangs, whose healing smart
Thy grace hath planted in my heart;
I know, I feel, Thy bounteous will!
Thou lovest me, Lord, Thou lovest me still!

76

Michaelmas Day.

Captain of God's host, whose dreadful might
Led forth to war the armed seraphim,
   And from the starry height,
   Subdued in burning fight,
Cast down that ancient dragon, dark and grim !

Thine angels, Christ ! we laud in solemn lays,
Our elder brethren of the crystal sky,
   Who, 'mid Thy glory's blaze,
   The ceaseless anthem raise,
And gird Thy throne in faithful ministry !

We celebrate their love, whose viewless wing
Hath left for us so oft their mansion high,
   The mercies of their King
   To mortal saints to bring,
Or guard the couch of slumbering infancy.

But Thee the First and Last, we glorify,
Who, when Thy world was sunk in death and sin,
   Not with Thine hierarchy,
   The armies of the sky,
But didst with Thine own arm the battle win.

Alone didst pass the dark and dismal shore,
Alone didst tread the wine-press, and alone.
   All glorious in Thy gore,
   Didst light and life restore,
To us who lay in darkness and undone !

Michaelmas Day.

    Therefore, with angels and archangels, we
To Thy dear love our thankful chorus raise,
    And tune our songs to Thee
    Who art, and art to be,
And endless as Thy mercies sound Thy praise!

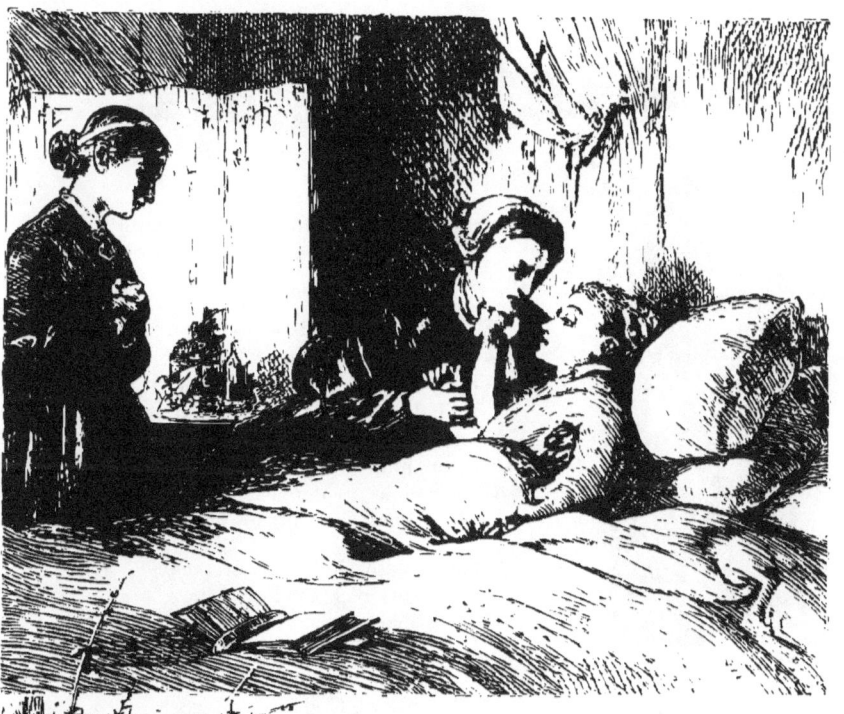

In Times of Distress and Danger,

H GOD, that madest earth and sky, the darkness and the day,
Give ear to this thy family, and help us when we pray !
For wide the waves of bitterness around our vessel roar,
And heavy grows the pilot's heart to view the rocky shore.

The cross our Master bore for us, for Him we fain would
    bear,
But mortal strength to weakness turns, and courage to
    despair !
Then mercy on our failings, Lord ! our sinking faith renew !
And when Thy sorrows visit us, oh send Thy patience too !

Before a Collection made for the Society for the Propagation of the Gospel.

FROM Greenland's icy mountains,
    From India's coral strand,
Where Afric's sunny fountains
    Roll down their golden sand ;
From many an ancient river,
    From many a palmy plain,
They call us to deliver,
    Their land from error's chain !

What though the spicy breezes
    Blow soft o'er Ceylon's isle,
Though every prospect pleases,'
    And only man is vile :
In vain with lavish kindness
    The gifts of God are strown,
The heathen in his blindness
    Bows down to wood and stone !

The following information regarding this universally admired hymn is transcribed from the fly-leaf accompanying the fac-simile of the original autograph (Hughes, Wrexham). The original was exhibited at the Great Exhibition of 1851, from Dr. Raffles collection :—

"On Whitsunday, 1819, the late Dr. Shipley, Dean of St. Asaph, and Vicar of Wrexham, preached a sermon in Wrexham Church, in aid of the Society for the Propagation of the Gospel in Foreign Parts. That day was also fixed for the commencement of the Sunday Evening Lectures, intended to be established in that Church, and the late Bishop of Calcutta (Heber), then Rector of Hodnet, the Dean's son-in-law, undertook to deliver the first lecture. In the course of the Saturday previous, the Dean and his son-in-law being together at the Vicarage, the former requested Heber to write 'Something for them to sing in the morning,' and he (Heber) retired for that purpose from the table, where the Dean and a few friends were sitting, to a distant part of the room. In a short time the Dean inquired, 'What have you written?' Heber having then

Propagation of the Gospel.

Can we, whose souls are lighted
　　With Wisdom from on high,
Can we to men benighted
　　The lamp of light deny?
Salvation! oh, Salvation!
　　The joyful sound proclaim,
Till each remotest nation
　　Has learn'd Messiah's name!

Waft, waft, ye winds, His story,
　　And you, ye waters, roll,
Till like a sea of glory
　　It spreads from pole to pole!
Till o'er our ransom'd nature,
　　The Lamb for sinner's slain,
Redeemer, King, Creator,
　　In bliss returns to reign!

composed the first three verses, read them over. ' There, there, that will do very well,' said the Dean; ' No, no, the sense is not complete,' replied Heber; accordingly he added the fourth verse, and the Dean being inexorable to his repeated request of ' Let me add another, oh! let me add another,' thus completed the Hymn of which the annexed is a fac-simile, and which has since become so celebrated. It was sung the next morning in Wrexham Church for the first time.— E."

A critic referring to the original autograph, writes:—

"*Ceylon*, in the second stanza, the disputed point, is the right and original reading. The whole hymn has but one correction: in the second stanza, *savage* has been written down first, and has then been softened down into *heathen*: in fact, the whole seems to have been what is commonly called 'an inspiration,' and has been written down by its gentle author ' wie aus einem Guss,' as the Germans have it. The handwriting is small, reminding one somewhat of that of Leigh Hunt though less delicate: and the last verse is written with a trembling hand, as if the writer had been deeply touched or affected by his subject."

Before the Sacrament.

— ⚜ —

BREAD of the world in mercy broken,
  Wine of the soul in mercy shed!
By whom the words of life were spoken,
  And in whose death our sins are dead!

Look on the heart by sorrow broken,
  Look on the tears by sinners shed,
And be Thy feast to us the token
  That by Thy grace our souls are fed!

An Introit to be sung between the Litany and Communion Service.

OH most merciful!
  Oh most bountiful!
God the Father Almighty;
By the Redeemer's
Sweet intercession
Hear us, help us when we cry!

Evening Hymn.

GOD that madest Earth and Heaven,
　　Darkness and Light!
Who the day for toil hast given,
　　For rest the night;
May Thine Angel guards defend us,
Slumber sweet Thy mercy send us,
Holy dreams and hopes attend us,
　　This livelong night!

At a Funeral.

— .• —

BENEATH our feet and o'er our head
 Is equal warning given ;
Beneath us lie the countless dead,
 Above us is the Heaven !

Their names are graven on the stone,
 Their bones are in the clay ;
And ere another day is gone,
 Ourselves may be as they.

At a Funeral.

Death rides on every passing breeze,
    He lurks in every flower:
Each season has its own disease,
    Its peril every hour!

Our eyes have seen the rosy light
    Of youth's soft cheek decay,
And fate descend in sudden night
    On manhood's middle day.

Our eyes have seen the steps of age
    Halt feebly towards the tomb,
And yet shall earth our hearts engage
    And dreams of days to come?

Turn, mortal, turn! thy danger know;
    Where'er thy foot can tread
The earth rings hollow from below,
    And warns thee of her dead!

Turn, Christian, turn! thy soul apply
    To truths divinely given;
The bones that underneath thee lie
    Shall live for Hell or Heaven!

At a Funeral.

—··

'THOU art gone to the grave! but we will not deplore thee,
  Though sorrows and darkness encompass the tomb;
Thy Saviour has pass'd through its portals before thee,
  And the lamp of His love is thy guide through the gloom!

Thou art gone to the grave! we no longer behold thee,
  Nor tread the rough path of the world by thy side;
But the wide arms of Mercy are spread to enfold thee,
  And sinners may die, for the SINLESS has died!

Thou art gone to the grave! and, its mansion forsaking,
  Perchance thy weak spirit in fear linger'd long;
But the mild rays of Paradise beam'd on thy waking,
  And the sound which thou heardst was the Seraphim's song!

Thou art gone to the grave! but we will not deplore thee,
  Whose God was thy ransom, thy guardian and guide;
He gave thee, He took thee, and He will restore thee,
  And death has no sting, for the Saviour has died!

On Recovery from Sickness.

OH Saviour of the faithful dead,
　　With whom Thy servants dwell,
Though cold and green the turf is spread
　　Above their narrow cell.

No more we cling to mortal clay,
　　We doubt and fear no more.
Nor shrink to tread the darksome way
　　Which Thou hast trod before!

'Twas hard from those I loved to go,
　　Who knelt around my bed,
Whose tears bedew'd my burning brow,
　　Whose arms upheld my head!

On Recovery from Sickness.

As fading from my dizzy view,
  I sought their forms in vain,
The bitterness of death I knew,
  And groan'd to live again.

'Twas dreadful when th' Accuser's power
  Assail'd my sinking heart,
Recounting every wasted hour,
  And each unworthy part.

But, Jesus! in that mortal fray,
  Thy blessed comfort stole,
Like sunshine in a stormy day,
  Across my darken'd soul!

When soon or late, this feeble breath
  No more to Thee shall pray,
Support me through the vale of death,
  And in the darksome way!

When cloth'd in fleshly weeds again
  I wait Thy dread decree,
Judge of the world! bethink Thee then,
  That Thou hast died for me.

LONDON: WILLIAM CLOWES AND SONS, STAMFORD STREET AND CHARING CROSS.

www.ingramcontent.com/pod-product-compliance
Lightning Source LLC
Chambersburg PA
CBHW022354020726

47500CB00002B/270